Whose Birthday Is It?

By Sherryl Clark

Illustrated by Jan Smith

Special thanks to our advisers for their expertise:

Adria F. Klein, Ph.D.
Professor Emeritus, California State University
San Bernardino, California

Susan Kesselring, M.A.
Literacy Educator
Rosemount-Apple Valley-Eagan (Minnesota) School District

PICTURE WINDOW BOOKS
Minneapolis, Minnesota

Levels for *Read-it!* Readers

- Familiar topics
- Frequently used words
- Repeating patterns

- New ideas
- Larger vocabulary
- Variety of language structures

- Challenges in ideas
- Expanded vocabulary
- Wide variety of sentences

- More complex ideas
- Extended vocabulary range
- Expanded language structures

A Note to Parents and Caregivers:

Read-it! Readers are for children who are just starting on the amazing road to reading. These beautiful books support both the acquisition of reading skills and the love of books.

The RED LEVEL presents familiar topics using common words and repeating sentence patterns.

The BLUE LEVEL presents new ideas using a larger vocabulary and varied sentence structure.

The YELLOW LEVEL presents more challenging ideas, a broad vocabulary, and wide variety in sentence structure.

The GREEN LEVEL presents more complex ideas, an extended vocabulary range, and expanded language structures.

When sharing a book with your child, read in short stretches, pausing often to talk about the pictures. Have your child turn the pages and point to the pictures and familiar words. And be sure to reread favorite stories or parts of stories.

There is no right or wrong way to share books with children. Find time to read with your child, and pass on the legacy of literacy.

Adria F. Klein, Ph.D.
Professor Emeritus
California State University
San Bernardino, California

First American edition published in 2005 by
Picture Window Books
5115 Excelsior Boulevard
Suite 232
Minneapolis, MN 55416
877-845-8392
www.picturewindowbooks.com

First published in Great Britain by Franklin Watts, 96 Leonard Street,
London, EC2A 4XD

Printed in the United States of America.

Library of Congress Cataloging-in-Publication Data
Clark, Sherryl.
Whose birthday is it? / by Sherryl Clark ; illustrated by Jan Smith.
p. cm. — (Read-it! readers)
Summary: Luke is worried that no one from his new school will come to his birthday
party, but when he and his parents inadvertently create a party mystery, everyone
is intrigued.
ISBN 1-4048-0554-0 (hardcover)
[1. Parties—Fiction. 2. Birthdays—Fiction.] I. Smith, Jan, 1956- ill. II. Title. III. Series.
PZ7.C55233Wh 2004
[E]—dc22
2004007624

It was a week until Luke's birthday. He wanted to have a party, but he had just moved to a new school.

He hadn't made any friends yet.

"Let's have a birthday party in the park," said Mom and Dad. "There are lots of places to play."

"I don't want a party," Luke said.

"No one will come."

But his parents didn't listen.

"I'll dress up as a clown," said Dad happily, "and do magic tricks."

"Yes, and I'll dress up as a fairy,"
added Mom. "I'll tell stories."

Mom and Dad helped Luke
write out party invitations for
everyone in his class.

10

That night, Luke cut "It's Luke's Birthday!" off the top of the invitations. All that was left was "Come to my party in the park!" and the date and time.

The next morning before class,
Luke put invitations on every
desk in his classroom.

He thought the other kids
would throw them away,
but they didn't!

"I wonder whose party it is," said Ray, looking for a name. "Maybe it's a movie star!" cried Amy excitedly.

"He wouldn't invite you then!" teased Thomas.

Luke was amazed. Everyone wanted to go to the party! It was a big, exciting mystery.

On Saturday, Mom and Dad got all the food ready. Then Mom dressed up as a fairy, and Dad dressed up as a clown.

They walked to the park, carrying the food for the party. People stared and smiled.

17

They spread the food out on a big
tablecloth. Mom and Dad sat
in the sun and waited.

Luke sneaked away and hid
behind some trees.

Then all the kids from Luke's
class walked into the park.

"Welcome," said the clown.

He gave a balloon to each child.

"Lovely to see you!" said the fairy.

She gave out candy and hats.

Soon everyone was playing games
and having a wonderful time.
They had forgotten it was
somebody's party.

They didn't know that the fairy and the clown were Luke's mom and dad.

Luke didn't want to hide anymore.

He wanted to have fun, too.

He joined in a balloon game.

He helped to find the treasure in
the treasure hunt. It was a box of
chocolates wrapped in gold paper.

The fairy brought out the birthday cake. Everyone said, "This is a great party. Whose birthday is it?" "Don't you know?" said the clown. "It's Luke's birthday!"

27

They all cheered when Luke blew
out the candles on his cake.

28

Then they gave him his
birthday presents.

But the best present for Luke was having so many new friends.

Levels for *Read-it!* Readers

**Read-it! Readers help children practice early reading
skills with brightly illustrated stories.**

Red Level: Familiar topics with frequently used words and
repeating patterns.

I Am in Charge of Me by Dana Meachen Rau
Let's Share by Dana Meachen Rau

Blue Level: New ideas with a larger vocabulary and a variety
of language structures.

At the Beach by Patricia M. Stockland
The Playground Snake by Brian Moses

Yellow Level: Challenging ideas with an expanded vocabulary
and a wide variety of sentences.

Flynn Flies High by Hilary Robinson
Marvin, the Blue Pig by Karen Wallace
Moo! by Penny Dolan
Pippin's Big Jump by Hilary Robinson
The Queen's Dragon by Anne Cassidy
Sounds Like Fun by Dana Meachen Rau
Tired of Waiting by Dana Meachen Rau
Whose Birthday Is It? by Sherryl Clark

Green Level: More complex ideas with an extended vocabulary
range and expanded language structures.

Clever Cat by Karen Wallace
Flora McQuack by Penny Dolan
Izzie's Idea by Jillian Powell
Naughty Nancy by Anne Cassidy
The Princess and the Frog by Margaret Nash
The Roly-Poly Rice Ball by Penny Dolan
Run! by Sue Ferraby
Sausages! by Anne Adeney
Stickers, Shells, and Snow Globes by Dana Meachen Rau
The Truth About Hansel and Gretel by Karina Law
Willie the Whale by Joy Oades

**A complete list of *Read-it!* Readers is available on our Web site:
www.picturewindowbooks.com**